CASTE OF THE MOUNTAIN

Prequel One - The Sunstone Saga

Nicolin Odel

CONTENTS

PART ONE

Chapter One

Home

Baal slammed his pickaxe into the stone, and sparks flew about him. He tensed his muscles and hammered the rock again. Sweat glistening from the thunderbolt tattoos atop his bald head. A hole collapsed inward, and a faint red light suddenly penetrated the dark mining cavern. Baal leaned in, scratching his ginger beard, peeking through the hole. *Still too much rubble.*

After some time, he had cleared a large enough hole to fit through. It connected to an even greater cavern. There stood an archway of black and green marble. A red cloud churned about where the doors would have been.

Baal immediately turned around and began filling in the hole he had dug. *What devilry is this?*

He nearly had all the rubble back in place when a voice questioned him, "What's this then, Foreman? What is the strange light?"

Baal turned to see his right-hand man, Alvar Kovaa. He was a short, stout man who waddled over and removed some dust-stained goggles. He squinted over a crooked nose at the newfound light. "Ha! By Teras' hammer, what could it be?"

"I need to clear more of this out," Baal answered inconspicuously, pointing at the debris. "But I do not like it. It is an ill omen for there to be light deep within the mountain."

I will tell no one of this strange gate.

"Ha!" the short man exclaimed, stubbly dirt-crusted face smiling with delight. "It could happen to be some new and precious material. Magical gemstones, perchance? Look, there is a chip of topaz here. The chieftain will wish to hear of this immediately."

"No, we could forget about it and continue in another direction. As a matter of fact, let us backtrack to the last intersection."

"You would give up such an opportunity for what? Superstition?" Alvar questioned, slanting a barely visible brow. "What do you fear?"

"I fear nothing!" Baal's voice boomed, echoing through the mine tunnels.

Alvar recoiled.

"Even so," Baal said as he ground his teeth. "I do not like this."

"There is no harm in having a look, Foreman Vasara. Seems like the gemstones are plentiful in this vein."

"Enough. Cover it up, and let us keep this between you and me, Alvar Kovaa?"

"Of course, of course, Foreman." Alvar repeatedly nodded.

Baal watched as Alvar covered the small hole with crushed stone and dust until the faint crimson light winked out of existence.

"Good. Time to surface," Baal said with a grunt. Then he removed a bell from a large pouch on the back of his belt. He rang it steadily as they sauntered on an incline through intersections and twisting tunnels. Other miners fell in behind them as they heard the bell calling for an end to the day's work. The chatter spilled about, growing and growing as miners, like ants, marched through the shafts.

"A feast is to be held in the chieftain's house. The ale will be flowing endlessly this night," one man said.

Another man rested a hand on Baal's shoulder. "Is not the feast in honor of your daughter's first hunt?"

Baal looked to see the only Auru who lived in Oitilla, Dominique Silvain, speaking to him. The young man, perhaps in his early twenties, was pale, once gangly, Aurulan-born. He had immigrated nearly two years ago and had become a part of their community. Baal had taken him under his wing as a miner, and he had bulked up quite a bit since his arrival. *He is a stout young lad now. But even so, Dom is still fragile and has much to learn.* "Indeed," Baal said with a toothy grin. "Not two days past my young flame staked a mountain bear through the heart as it charged down on her."

"Teras' might," Dominique exclaimed in perfect Vouri dialect. "You could have Hata shoot an iron-horned sheep or a snow fox. You Vasaras are incredibly ridiculous."

"Not only House Vasara, but it is the Vouri way," Baal grunted. "We Vouri are a proud people, a resilient people. We mine the stone, shape the metal, brave the cold, and win in battle. It is the way of the mountain. The way of Teras."

"Ridiculous..." Dom sighed, then scurried ahead, calling back over his shoulder, "Tell Hata I *desperately* look forward to seeing her at the feast later. Farwell for now, Baal."

Tell her yourself, boy, or you will never walk the mountain. By Teras's stones, Aurulan people are so strange, Baal pondered as he followed slowly. Exiting the main mine tunnel into a slightly brighter light. Into the cave town of Oitilla, the city was recessed into the mountainside. The sun sparkled through a massive pillar of frozen water at the outside center of the village. *Ice Pillar Falls.* An icy plateau spread out from the waterfall's base and over the far cliff. The log homesteads and longhouses sheltered beneath the cavernous mountaintop, like resting on a tongue of a massive gaping maw.

Baal took a deep breath through his nose; the tinge of iron smoke from the forges and the succulent juice of roasting meat washed over him. He turned for home as his stomach grumbled. Tucked away in the corner of the cave town, he came to his house. The L-shaped log homestead was simple, surrounded by a short picket fence to keep his two goats in. The names of his ancestors were carved into the wall of the logs above and around the entryway.

He entered and spread his arms wide. "My mate! I am home."

Brena Vasara turned from where she was heating water in a large steel tub and smiled warmly at her husband. She came to him, and they held one another for a long moment. As tall as he, her long blonde hair hung loose behind, brushing the floor. Her chain mail, sword, and shield rested on a chair next to the bath, only her under wraps still clothing her. The matching black thunderbolt tattoos stormed across her body from head to toe.

"*Vaimoni,*" Baal whispered.

"*Aviomieheni,*" Brena answered as she pressed her lips to his. She sighed as their lips departed. "Now, into the bath with you. We must be clean and in our best furs for Hata's feast tonight."

Baal's eyes strayed toward a pot bubbling over the hearth. "A little grub is all I need. I will join you in a moment." He let go of his wife and walked toward the delicious-smelling food.

"Be quick. Hata will be home soon should you wish for a quick mountain stroll."

Baal halted. *Teras' fortitude. I want both.* Then shrugged. "Mate, I am famished. One bowl, and I will wash your back. Besides"—he grinned mischievously—"if we are to drink at the feast tonight, I suspect to walk the mountains with you many times this night."

Brena snorted as she finished undressing and stepped into the large tub. It was large enough for three or four people to fit into comfortably.

Ice was cut and hulled from the plateau lake to be boiled in massive metal cauldrons at the crossroads of each living section. Supplying his and the other homes around it with the much-needed water.

Baal was fervently scarfing down the bowl of stew when the door swung open behind him. His daughter, Hata Vasara, strode in, carrying a bag of wheat flour.

"By the mountain, flour has gone up in price again. Those Aurulan traders are gouging us." Hata huffed, dropping the sack near the table and sitting down, stretching her long legs. A bead of sweat dripped from her fire-red hair down her forehead. Her gaze fell on Brena washing in the bath. "Oh gods, I could use one myself."

Brena's eyes met Baal, a smile behind them as if to say, *now you will have to wait.* Baal simply grinned back at her and, with a grunt, said, "Go then, *tyttäreni.* You must make ready for the feast. I will soil the bath once you two are clean as plucked chickens."

"Oh, come on, *Isä.*" Hata laughed. "I will wash *Äiti's* back, and she can wash yours."

"I agree with Hata," Brena said. "Be quick. The water is cooling, and the feast is waiting."

With that, Baal and Hata joined Brena in the large round tub. Baal growled or *purred* as Brena used the rough wash rag to scrape his back, his large arms unable to reach the particular spot.

Hata poured water over her mother's long hair and scrubbed the thyme-scented wood-ash soap into the blonde locks. After rinsing the soap, she sat leisurely in the bath with a brush and combed her mother's hair.

Sufficiently clean, they pulled the stopper from the base of the tub and the water drain into a trench along the floor and out into the back lane. Steam wafted as the warm water met cool air.

Baal put on his finest snow-wolf hide pauldron and cleanest leather tunic. He rubbed his bald head. *The damned women's hair causes seconds to turn to minutes, and the next thing, the sun has set.* He then sat and grabbed another bowl of stew while waiting for the two women to finish getting ready.

Hata braided her mother's tresses into a traditional triple plait tight against her crown. Hata's hair was relatively short, not quite to her chin. It didn't take long to brush it. Brena then helped Hata into her newly tanned mountain-bear hide cloak. Hata grimaced as the weight of the animal's heavy fur and skull hung upon her.

"Be strong, my daughter," Baal reassured. "Remember, you slew this beast with your own two hands, and we honor you tonight."

"You lured the bear in, Father. All I did was hold the pike," Hata mumbled.

"You made the killing blow. You flourished in the hunt."

"A mountain bear is no small feat for a pack of hunters with hounds, my daughter," Brena added. "My first hunt did not provide me such a mighty foe. The mountain cat was starving and weak when I came upon it."

"Ah ha." Baal laughed. "Do you remember our first hunt together, my mate? We snuck up on the *giant raptor* nesting on the anvil's peak."

"Voitooon! That was a battle!" Brena praised. "The vulture was protecting its fledglings. We ate well that night, and the blood lust of battle had us *sprinting* the mountain. I think that night was when our dear daughter was conceived."

"Oh, Teras, aid me." Hata moaned with embarrassment. "Let us go. We will be late for my own feast."

Baal shrugged and grunted. "I've been ready for half a bell."

Brena jabbed him playfully with a fist as they departed their home.

Chapter Two

FEAST

The sound of revelry cascaded over them as they pushed open the massive doors into the village chief's longhouse. Wood carvings of great warriors watching them enter the threshold. A long firepit lined the center of the longhouse, extended tables on each side crowded with townsfolk, already well into eating and drinking to their heart's content. There were doors to separate chambers on either side, and the chieftain's living quarters resided behind where he sat at the far end of the hall.

Chieftain Ota Vastaan stood as Baal and Brena flanked their daughter's entrance. "The guest of honor arrives." Ota's voice thundered out over the course, and everyone quieted. "Hata Vasara, victorious in her first hunt. *Voitoon!*"

"*Voitoon!*" The crowd erupted.

Hata smiled as she was led around one side of the room; people stood congratulating her and wishing her the might of Teras as she went. Baal's pride in his daughter grew as they approached the empty seats on the right-hand side nearest the chieftain's table.

"Sit! Sit. My honored guests." Ota gestured extravagantly to the seats. His graying blonde hair was crested with an iron circlet with rubies around it. His thick blonde beard shook as he seated himself with a laugh. "Ha ha. Vasara, your noble name echoes on the mountain this night. Feast and be merry." He waved, and two serving women tapped one of the three massive kegs that made up one wall of the building. They placed the foaming tankard of dark *Vouri* ale before the three guests.

Baal stood and lifted his tankard. "*Voitoon*, friends. My *tyttäreni*, Hata of House Vasara, by the strength of Teras, bested the mountain bear not a few days past. Anyone who can out-drink me this night and stay standing, I offer one favor from my house to yours!" He raised the tankard further and shouted, "For this, we feast!"

"RAH!" The cheer echoed and nearly shook the joyous longhouse.

Baal sat and began unceremoniously gnawing on a fat roasted duck leg. *By Teras stones, I am famished.*

After some time and a few drinks, Ota leaned toward the trio. "A fine toast for a fine family." He paused for a long moment, eyeing Baal. "An *honest* family."

Baal feigned ignorance, giving a duck-filled, toothy grin in response. But his eyes scanned the room as he did so. He found Alvar Kovaa at the far side, hunched behind a rowdy group of warriors, trying as he might to be unseen by Baal. *Cannot keep your tongue between your lips, serpent, Alvar Kovaa.*

"What are you implying, Chieftain?" Brena asked sternly. "Are you accusing House Vasara of dishonesty? You would reproach our honor?" Brena's voice elevated as she spoke, neck reddening.

"Your mate did not tell you?" Ota scoffed. "Apparently, dishonesty has its roots deep within House Vasara already."

"What is he talking about, Baal?" Brena asked, her face flushing further.

"I have not even had time to think," Baal grunted. "Let alone speak of my finding in the mine. Let us meet in private tomorrow, Ota. Tonight is not the night for strife."

I will not speak of what I saw down there.

"You would keep this knowledge to yourself and skulk into the mines in the dark of night and steal from me?" Ota stood, slamming his tankard to the table. "Steal from the Vouri?"

Brena and Baal also leaped up, glaring back at the chieftain in defiance. Muscles tensing in anticipation. An eerie quiet held the room captive.

Hata cowered further into her chair, sipping her mug of ale.

"Joo," Baal said, taking a breath to calm himself. "There was an abnormal finding in the deepest depths of the mines. Something that is not of Teras. Something that is *not* of the mountain."

"It has to be a vein of magical gems, Lord Chieftain," Alvar called from the other end of the room. "Or even an equivalent to the rare *volframi* ore."

"You dishonor our word, Alvar Kovaa." Baal opposed, trying as he may to keep his anger in check. "You will no longer work in Foreman Vasara's mine."

Ota slammed his fist into the table. "That is not for you to say. Alvar has been loyal to his chieftain, loyal to all the Vouri."

Grumbles of agreement rippled through the onlookers.

"Whatever is down there is dangerous." Baal pleaded. "What could give such an outlandish crimson glow so deep within the mountain? It is an ill omen."

Others murmured, nodding their heads at Baal's distress.

Brena whispered in Baal's ear, "I should have liked to know of this before being slandered in front of our people, oh mate of mine."

"I am sorry." He returned her quiet words. "I was hungry, and I was still pondering over it."

"You are always hungry." Brena sighed. "But it is alright, *vaimoni*. At any rate, we cannot let them insult our name further. Do you want Ota or Alvar?"

Baal glowered at Alvar, who had broken his word. *I wish to break his bones and give him back to Teras.*

The still dust-covered man shrank back under Baal's stare.

The crooked bastard did not even bathe for the feast. But Baal's burning glare then turned to Ota. He sucked the rage between his teeth and bellowed, "Ota Vastaan! Only you would smear our house with your feeble words. I challenge you for throwing affront upon our name!"

Ota stood and cracked his knuckles and then his neck. From next to his chair, he lifted a massive war hammer. Blue-tinged metal, with runes inscribed along the shaft and head. Only the Chieftain of the Vouri could wield this weapon. Raising the heavy war hammer above his head, he shouted, "I accept Baal Vasara's right to challenge. At dusk tomorrow, we shall air our grievance in battle."

"The stakes?!" someone called out.

"Baal for Chieftain!" another shouted.

"Hail Ota, long may he reign!"

The room vented in turmoil as two factions formed, the first consisting mainly of miners on the side of Baal. The second was of the rowdy young warriors to the side of Ota Vastaan. They shouted and insulted across the feast hall at one another.

"Enough!" Ota brought the hammer down in a mighty swing, crushing the table before him in two. Food and drink crashed to the ground. Ota's mate, a slight, quiet young woman, yelped and retreated away from the destruction. Ota came before Baal, spitting his words in his face. "By Teras's justice, should you become the victor and strike me down, by all means, take up the mantel of chieftain! But should you lose?" Ota hissed. "House Vasara is no longer of the Vouri."

Gasps and cheers burst as Ota Vastaan called for a scribe to have the challenge chiseled in stone. A rickety old man hobbled out, placed a large stone tablet on one of the tables, and began chiseling away.

By the will of Teras, Baal prayed. *The stakes are now set in the very mountain He grew.*

"Wait!" Brena shouted over the turmoil, unsheathing her longsword and leveling it at Alvar Kovaa. "For breaking his word, I challenge House Kovaa to the same fate."

Another cheer erupted as Alvar sputtered and stammered in horror. No words were heard from his mouth as the scribe chiseled his name into the stone tablet.

Chapter Three

REVEAL

Hata found her friends in an adjacent chamber, having retreated from the turmoil and rising tensions in the main room. Two young men were wrestling in the center of the room, trying desperately to push each other out of the ring made of soft sandy shale. Young women giggled as they watched, and other young men readied themselves, expanding their shirtless chests and flexing as they awaited their turns.

Hata slid in on a bench next to Silja Vastaan, the chieftain's wife and Hata's finest friend. They were both the same age at twenty summers old and had grown up together. Silja was Ota's third wife. The first had died in childbirth, and the second mysteriously got sick when she bore no children. Many townsfolk whisper that Ota Vastaan was cursed and doomed to have no heir. But he had chosen Silja, honoring her house to be made the wife of the mighty village chieftain. She had yet to come with babe.

Silja turned to Hata as she nuzzled in close. Silja's brunette hair fell around her face just past her shoulders. Immediately, upon seeing Hata, tears filled Silja's hazelnut eyes. "Ota is going to kill your father and banish you from Oitilla. I will never see you again."

"Ha," Hata hooted, pressing her forehead to Silja's. "My father is more than a match for that old man. He will not lose to a geezer such as Ota."

Silja brushed Hata's red hair from her face and behind her ear. "But if he does win…"

"Don't think about it, Sil. I won't leave."

There was a shout from the boys wrestling. Hata's eyes met Dominque Silvain's, the Auru. He smiled broadly at her as he entered the ring. *Ever since he came here, he has been trying to impress me. Every day, he pesters me. Well, him, and all the other boys of age.* Hata groaned internally.

"Go back to Nidhaut, little flower," his opponent called. *What was his name again?* Hata recalled. *Yes, Roope, that's right.*

Dominque was shorter than Roope, his tall Vouri contender. Yet Dom had a stockiness to his shoulders, a tension. A miner's arms.

Suddenly, they were in motion. Dom charged in, bent low, grasping at the other's long legs.

Roope grunted as Dom's shoulder thudded into his waist. Wrapping his arms around Dom from above and behind, Roope's face went pink, straining to pull the Auru off him.

Dom's feet were planted, one forceful step forward at a time, pushing the tall one closer to the ring's edge.

Roope hissed in rage and struck Dom in the side with a fist.

Dominque faltered.

Another blow hit him on the other side.

Cheers from the on-looking Vouri boys chorused the room.

"Striking is not part of the match!" Hata yelled, but was simply ignored.

"Leave them be, Hata. Let us get out of here," Silja whispered. "Just the two of us."

I can't let them get away with that, not to anybody. Hata stood and pushed to the front. "Stop beating him, Roope! Where is your dignity?"

"Auru bastard," Roope hissed as he lifted his fist again.

Suddenly, Dom's foot fixed in and behind Roope's leg, and Dom's muscles tensed as he twisted. Roope thudded to the ground, head lulling back with the impact. Half his body outside the ring.

"*Voitoon!*" Dominque shouted.

There was stunned silence from the on-looking boys.

"*Voitoon*, Dom!" Hata answered the call as she rushed to him, pulling his arm around her shoulder, and walking him slowly out of the ring. She fumbled over the words, asking in the Aurulan dialect, "Are you hurt?" He had been tutoring Hata's family in the Aurulan language since he arrived.

He winced as she lifted him, as she was half a head taller. "We can speak Vouri." He chuckled. "At any rate, should I be challenging him to a deathmatch now as well?"

"Teras's stones, no, silly Auru," Hata said. "You would surely die if you did."

She sat Dom down on the bench where Silja and she had just been seated. Silja was nowhere in sight. Hata looked about. *Is she upset with me?*

"Thank you, Hata," Dominque said, putting a thumb to his lips in the Primus One's prayerful gesture.

Hata was still not used to seeing Primus One dogma and the litanies of his subordinate gods in Oitilla. Skrull, Hettra, Qav, Urasil, and Thetren are the more dominant of the lesser gods. *Who could believe the far-fetched tales Dom has told me about? Teras is the only true god.*

"Hata?"

"Sorry, Dom," Hata started. "What were you saying?"

"I was thanking you and asking if you would like to walk with me?"

"You mean to walk the mountain?" Hata snorted.

"Oh no, no!" Dom became bright red. "Do you, Vouri, not simply spend time talking and walking like normal people?"

"Ha!" Hata stifled a laugh. "Vouri talk. We drink, and we talk. We fight, and we talk."

"Ah, I see"—he hesitated—"then can we get a drink and chat? Then once we get to know each other, perhaps we could walk the moun—"

Hata sighed audibly. *He is a nice boy, but they all want the same thing. He's even cute in a way with his fair Auru skin. Almost feminine. Silja is far lovelier. Where is Silja? I need to find her.* "I'm sorry, Dom, I like you and enjoy your stories. I would drink with you, but Silja is distressed and needs me. Not tonight, but perhaps another time we can drink and talk?"

His shoulders fell somewhat as he leaned back against the wall, hand on his ribs. His face became sullen, lips in a hard line. "Very well, Hata Vasara, another time then." He closed his eyes.

She took that as a dismissal and hurried away to find Silja. *I wager she is in her regular hiding place.* Hata took a back door out of the room into the brisk night. Her breath fogged as she went to the large stables adjacent to the chieftain's edifices. Horses and mules whined as Hata pulled open the doors and slid inside the smelly animal-warmed interior. From there, she climbed the stairs to the second-level loft. Silja sat in the hay, cradling a newborn ratting hound pup. The mother bitch lay nursing a litter, nuzzled in the corner of a makeshift nest.

"I thought I'd find you here, Sil," Hata said as she sat down beside Silja. "Why did you run away?"

Silja turned her head to Hata. Her eyes and cheek were red from weeping. "You were so focused on that boy from Aurulan. I did not want to get in your way."

"Dom?" Hata snorted. "He's my father's ward of sorts, under the guidance of House Vasara. He's teaching me Auru. There's nothing between us."

"On Teras's peak," Silja said through a sniffle. "You speak the truth?"

"Of course, friend Silja."

"Even so, with your father's honor duel, things will never be the same between us."

"Oh, Sil, I told you not to worry about that. When *isä* defeats your mate, you will be rid of that old man for good."

Silja's eyes soften. "You really think so? I won't have to please that old hand a day longer?"

"Yes, Sil, now come here." Hata embraced Silja, their cheeks pressed together. Silja pushed in closer, nearly burying into Hata's skin and causing them to fall into the hay. They both giggled as Silja stared down into Hata's eyes. Silja's gaze then fixed on Hata's lips, and before Hata could protest, Silja kissed her softly.

What is this? Hata's eyes widened in shock that her friend would kiss her like this. Yet there was something, excitement, a spark of magnetism butterflying about Hata's stomach. *It feels so right.*

Silja began to pull away at Hata's surprised expression.

Hata put a hand up around the back of Silja's head and held their lips together, passionately returning the kiss. Moments of pure pleasure engulfed them.

Silja maneuvered her body atop Hata's, cradling Hata's face in her hands as they caressed.

"Silja!" Ota Vastaan's voice echoed from outside the doors of the stable barn.

Silja scrambled away from Hata. "Oh no, oh no. He wants me. He will take out his anger from arguing with your parents on me tonight."

"Then do not go. Stay with me."

"He will find me. If I wait any longer, it will only get worst." Silja readjusted her dress and descended the stairs, saying, "Goodbye, Hata. I wish I could stay with you forever." Her head disappeared, and Hata heard the door groan open and then shut. A cold chill blew in momentarily.

Hata shivered, alone in the loft. She lay back in the hay, thoughts of Silja's tender lips, stunning eyes, their bodies pressing into one another...*I wish that, too, Silja. After all these years growing up together, how are these feelings only revealed to me now? After tomorrow's battle, it will be forever.*

Chapter Four

TAINT

Brena Vasara stood upon the table and drained the tankard down her gullet. "Is there anyone else?!" she called out across the room. The feast had receded. Baal had long since fallen from his bench and lay snoring contently. A sparse few moaned and groaned as they bent their heads to the table or passed out on the floor. Others stumbled out the doors into the night to vomit or seek out their warm homes.

Brena sighed, teetering as she stepped down from the tabletop. Muttering to herself, "What a lot of yellowbellies."

"One more drink?" someone asked from behind.

She whirled about, grinning wickedly, ready to take on the new challenger. Anger boiled up as she saw the face of Alvar Kovaa before her, a smug smile upon it. He held a tankard in each hand.

"In honor of our duel, shall we drink together?" he reiterated, holding out one of the tankards.

Brena exhaled, fatigue beginning to overcome all else. She took the mug and sat. "Alvar, why did you sully our name? Baal has always treated you as his second."

He sat across from her and took a long draught.

Brena did likewise, the ale cooling her mood further.

"It is Teras' truth, it is. Baal is a respectable foreman. He oversees the mines well." Alvar grieved and took another drink. "Yet, at times, he is superstitious and mingy."

Brena downed the remains of the tankard, gulping vigorously as Alvar spoke.

"A bad omen in the middle of the earth? It could be nothing more than a shaft of light seeping down to cast a reflection on some rubies or other such gemstones?"

Brena tried to focus on the man, her vision blurring slightly.

"There is no harm in exploring the shaft. Our chieftain understands. I tell you, those gems would catch a pretty pence in Nidhaut."

Pain gripped and twisted in her gut. She stood abruptly, and vertigo caused her to stumble as she walked toward the massive main doors.

"It would seem as if I am the victor in the contest of drink," Alvar's words were distant and muffled. "Sweet dreams."

She gasped as the frigid mountain air blasted against her. Then a wave of nausea caused her to lurch over and vomit, after which she could not move. She could not think straight, and her body did not respond.

Hata pulled the rickety old cart she regularly used to gather her parents after a long night of feasting up to the front doors of the longhouse. She tilted her head curiously as a body lay huddled outside the massive gates. The wood-carved warriors kept watch over the drunkard. *What fool would pass out in this freezing cold?* Hata thought as she rolled the body over to see who it was. Her mother stared lifelessly up into nothingness.

"*Äiti*!" Hata cried in terror. "Mother!"

Hata summoned all her strength as she dragged her mother back toward the longhouse. "Wake up! You cannot be dead!" Leaning against the great doors, she *pushed*. Her eyes fell on her father, sleeping contently as warmth greeted her.

She let out a blood-curdling scream, "*Isä*!"

Baal's eyes shot open. He leaped up and rushed to them. "What is wrong, *tyttäreni*? *Vaimoni*?" He took Brena in his arms and cradled her, shaking her gently. "*Brena*!"

Blotches of red were forming on Brena's skin. Hata shook her head. "Shush for a moment." She leaned in close to her mother's mouth. The faintest of short sucking breaths could be heard. "She is still breathing. We must take her to the healer's hut."

Without hesitation, Baal lifted his spouse effortlessly from the floor and began to run. Hata followed closely, catching a glimpse of a man in the shadows of a far corner of the longhouse as they rushed back into the bitter darkness of night.

The healer's hut was on the edge of town on a small overlook of the frozen plateau lake. Steps had been carved into the stone leading up to the homestead. Baal took them two at a time as he bound upward. Hata had fallen behind. She came to the bottom stair as her father crested the top. Gasping for air, Hata slowly climbed after him. When she finally reached the top, Baal had already disappeared into the round, skin-hide structure. It consisted of three connected domes with smoke puffing gently out the two outer domes through openings in their centers.

Hata pushed the fur-hide door aside and entered the dimly lit chamber. Bones rattled, and dried herbs crackled as she moved further into the room. A cauldron bubbled in the center over a low fire. Baal knelt at Brena's side as the old healer woman hobbled over with a large bearskin blanket.

Seeing Hata standing there, the old woman thrust the fur into her hands. "Ho there, girl. Cover her, then fetch more water to boil. There is a bucket over there." A crooked finger pointed. In the depictions of feathers and fangs, the woman's tattoos on her face were cracked and faded from age.

Hata had rarely seen or spoken to the old healer and stood gawking, the fur covering clutched in her arms.

"Now!" the healer barked, then turned. Her dark feathered cloak disappeared into the second chamber.

"Do as she says, my daughter," Baal said, still cradling his spouse.

Hata, startled, quickly tucked her mother into the thick gray-black fur hide. "Teras's fortitude, Mother." She kissed Brena gently on the forehead. "Right, I will go fetch the water."

"Ho boy, leave her there and come with me, Baal Vasara," the old crone, Niemela, beckoned him.

He gently lay Brena down by the fire. *She is warm now.* He stood and followed the healer into the second dome of the hut. There was an odd light emanating from a lantern. A yellow light. A tender light. Plants grew and blossomed throughout the room. Rich soil encompassed the entirety of the chamber, and vines grew up makeshift trellis while others spread out, creeping along the ground. Bees buzzed, and spiders made large webs between plants.

"How can anything grow here?" Baal questioned. "Nothing grows this far up the mountain."

"You are correct, young Vasara," Niemela said as she shuffled through some clay pots on a small table. "There are secrets that must be kept, that must not leave this chamber."

"If it does not dishonor my name, then have at it."

She held out a shaking gaunt open hand. Her fingers seemed unable to straighten correctly.

Baal squinted, barely seeing the tiny black seed on her palm.

Niemela unsteadily placed her other hand over the seed, and the same faint glow of the lantern flowed through her fingers. She pulled her hand away, and a young sprout perched perilously in the open palm. She crouched and planted it in the earth, then renewed her hands around it, the light warming the chamber.

"You are magi? Like the Auru, Dominque, has said to me. He told me the stories of their great council of chirping birds."

"Indeed, boy, that is why we keep this secret. Why all the Vouri keeps this secret. Should it get out into the Earste Lân, my days would be numbered."

"Let them come"—Baal snorted—"and feel the might of the Vouri."

"Ho boy, yet a juvenile. But never mind that. Did you come here to speak politics or preserve your mate?"

"My Brena. *Joo.* What must we do, wise one?"

"This." Again, she pulled her hands away, and an entire grown plant was below. It was a shrub with spiked evergreen foliage and pink flowers blossoming. She snipped a few of the flowers and returned to the table. She took Baal's aid and instructed him to crush the flowers into a fine grain with mortar and pestle. She then took a small stick of charcoal and added it to the mixture. Baal quickly turned the pink paste into a dark crimson muck. Finally, she moved the contents to a larger steel pot and added honey and wine.

Baal nodded in fascination as he prayed silently. *By Teras's fortitude, let this magi's concoction save my Brena.*

"Mandrake or bloodroot?" Niemela grumbled.

"What are you muttering about, healer?"

"Poisons," Niemela snorted. "Do you not see that Brena was poisoned?"

He'd been trying not to think about it. *I only want to save my Brena!* He tried to think about why someone would do this, but nothing came to him. His mind was too focused on his mate, who lay in a death state a few steps away. He simply whispered, "Why?"

"It must have something to do with your honor-bound contests—"

"Hello? Anyone there?" Hata's voice came from the other chamber.

"Good, good, let us return," the crone wheezed, hobbling forward. "It is nearly ready."

Baal followed her back into the chamber to see Hata soaking a rag and placing it on Brena's brow.

"Ho girl, you have brought the water then? Add some to this." Niemela placed the pot with the medicine mixture on the fire near Brena.

Hata nodded and carefully poured some water into the vessel. It didn't take long for the mixture to begin boiling as the water had been fetched from one of the ice-melt cauldrons in town and was still quite warm.

Nearly as soon as it did begin boiling, the healer woman removed it from the heat. Then she filled a small, wooden cup with the brew. Hands still shaking, she held the cup out to Hata. "Here now, girl, your hands are steadier than mine. Have her drink what she can."

Hata's eyes met his. Baal nodded and lifted Brena to a half-seated position in his arms, while Hata held the cup to her lips. At first, Brena would not take it, her face stonelike; the brew dripping down her chin.

The old crone heaved a sigh and leaned over Hata's shoulder; her bony hands then pinched Brena's jaw. Niemela grimaced in pain as she commanded, "Now, girl!"

Brena coughed and spluttered, then took a large gulp. Then another bout of coughing racked her. Little had she finished the fit when the old crone nudged Hata to give her more.

His daughter looked apprehensive but did as she was bid.

This time, Brena drank deeply. After draining the cup and another refill, they heard her weakened voice come to them in a hoarse whisper, "Baal?"

"Ho now, she needs rest. Lay her back down, and I will tend to her through what remains of the night."

"I will stay," Baal grunted.

"I will too," Hata exclaimed.

"This is not an inn." Niemela shook her head. "Teras's damned pups these days, doing whatever so they please."

"I will not leave my mate," Baal rumbled.

"Brena Vasara will be fine. Look, her face already has more color to it now." Niemella groaned. "At any rate, the sun is nearly up. Do you not have a duel to prepare for this day? Or so I've heard."

"You know about that?" Hata questioned curiously.

"I know of all happenings in Oitilla." Niemela fixed her gaze upon Baal's daughter. "Some would check how far they take certain *friendships*."

Baal laughed. "My daughter would not walk the mountain with an Auru. Though she is free to do as she pleases."

Hata's cheeks flushed. "You both do not know anything. I'm going home to try to get some sleep."

Baal watched his daughter storm out of the little room. He shrugged, shoulders still shaking with a slight chuckle. "I do not understand your sex, Healer Niemela."

The hunched woman ushered him out the door, muttering, "Ho Teras, why did you provide us with such solid skulls for men?"

INTEGRITY

Silja Vastaan squirmed out from under her mate's massive arm. Ota Vastaan had huffed and lashed about drunkenly, dragging her back to their bed, but had passed out before he could even kick his trousers off. *I'll only have a few bruises tomorrow.*

She slipped out of bed, donning a thick white fur cloak, and tiptoed through the feast hall, past sleeping drunkards, and into the morning air. *Perhaps Hata is awake. Does she hate me for kissing her? We have been friends since childhood. I pray to Teras that this does not end that friendship. Yet I have dreamed of becoming more than childhood friends for some time.*

Silja basked in the memory of their mouths pressed together in a union. That sweetened sensual stroke of their tongues...*What more could we explore together?* She nearly walked into the door of the Vasara homestead, not realizing she'd been daydreaming as she walked.

She knocked softly. No answer. She knocked louder, and still, no one came. She gently pushed the door open. No one was in the main room with the hearth, furniture and the massive steel tub at one end. Silja crept to the other side of the home and peeked into the sleeping chambers through a deer hide curtain. Hata and her father were fast asleep in the two beds that made up the chamber. She went and sat beside Hata on the smaller of the two beds. She stared down at the sleeping woman. *By Teras's might! She is beautiful.* Silja gently brushed Hata's hair behind her ear with her fingers.

Hata moaned and stirred.

Silja leaned close to her ear and whispered, "I love you."

Hata moaned again but did not open her eyes.

I should let her sleep. They must have had a long night.

Silja gazed at Hata for a lengthy while, fantasizing about lying beside her, holding her from behind. Turning Hata about and kissing her, their clothing mystically removed.

Hata's father snorted and choked on a snore, startling Silja. *Oh gods, I need to get back before Ota wakes up demanding to break his fast.* She gathered herself and hurried back out into the stone streets of Oitilla. Stopping at the single bakehouse that was always up early preparing the day's bread.

Hata awoke to the sound of a shout outside. *By the gods, it must be late!* She sprang out of bed and sprinted out. There was a gathering of people in the center road surrounding her father.

"My mate was poisoned!" Baal bellowed out into the crowd. "Ota Vastaan heaves shit upon his honor and attempts to murder my Brena!"

The crowd about Baal erupted.

"Let us bring him to justice!"

"String him up and flog him!"

"Baal for chieftain!"

They began moving as a mob toward the town center and the chieftain's longhouse. Baal swept up in their midst.

"Isä!" Hata called out to her father.

His eyes caught hers, and he pointed in the direction of the healer's hut, mouthing the words to check on Brena.

She quickly returned inside as the crowd dispersed and grabbed a loaf of hard bread. She began chewing it as she started out again.

Dom stood outside the fence gate, waiting for her. "Hata Vasara!" he greeted cheerfully. "Shall we follow the turmoil bound to burst at the chieftain's?"

"I cannot. I must go to the healer's hut and tend to my mother."

"Hettra's mercy, I'm sorry. How is she doing?"

Irritation grated on Hata's wits as Dom annoyed her, and something snapped within her. "I do not know. Just leave me be."

He opened his mouth as he began to say something else, but it stayed open in silent shock.

"By the mountain. I am sorry, Dom." Hata sighed. "It has been hectic day and night, and I need to focus."

His mouth formed that same hard line as the night before, and his eyes glistened as he turned wordlessly away.

"Dom, I said I was sorry."

He hurried away and did not look back.

Blasted boys. Acting like Teras's damned children. Hata stomped away in a rage to Niemela's hut. *I wish Silja was with me.*

That bastard poisoned my Brena. I will kill him. I will make him suffer. Baal's fury grew as the mob hollered and stormed toward the longhouse. His right-hand grip tightened on his massive pickaxe as he hefted a large round shield on his left.

The mob cheered as they marched. Pounding on doors as they went.

"Baal Vasara has been wronged! We march to cast down our malicious chieftain!"

He will die by my hand. Baal's teeth audibly screeched together.

Ota Vastaan stood on the threshold of his lodge. Two hands resting on the pommel of the runic war hammer at his feet. He grinned as he caught sight of Baal and the crowd ushering him to the forefront.

Baal could see nothing but red as Ota opened his mouth and said something. Bala did not hear the words. With a roar, he charged. Pickaxe held high, aimed at the skull of Ota Vastaan.

Brena dreamed of days past. The days when they were young. Baal had been oblivious to her forward desires and attempts to court him. She would wait for him at the entrance to the mines with a basket of food at the end of the day. Food was how she crept into his heart.

"Ah, Brena Laakso," Baal exclaimed with a smile, his face caked with dust and soil.

"Baal Vasara," she nodded in return.

"The usual spot?"

"Joo."

In the warmer months, they would follow a small mountain trail down the slopes into a pine and birch wooded glen, the meltwater of the frozen plateau trickling in a stream before them. Birds sang, and bees buzzed around the new wildflower growth. They would sit and eat and speak about their days.

"How goes your training?" Baal grunted through a mouthful of pork.

"I am to be promoted to thegn," Brena said proudly. "Old man Isto says I am a match for any man in our warrior ranks."

"*Voitoon*! This is good tidings."

"How goes it in the mines?"

"A new vein of iron was discovered, so we have our work cut out for us."

Brena inched closer, so she was leaning against him. He kept eating and did not seem to take notice. *Perhaps he will get a hint today.*

He gulped down some ale and belched. "*Rah*. My stomach is filled."

She leaned close to his ear. "There is something else here you could fill."

He turned and looked at her, then down at the basket. "There is a bit of pork roast left if you are still hungry, Brena."

She closed her eyes in disbelief...

Brena blinked her crusted eyes open. The pain coursing through her body had lessened, but she was still chilled to the bone.

"Ho there, lass, it awakens." A reedy old voice rang in Brena's ears.

"Where am I? What happened?"

"You were poisoned. Not to mention saturated on ale," the old woman said.

What is her name again? Niemale? Niemela?

"Too much drink only weakens the body when fighting a sickness," Niemela continued.

What? Poisoned? By who? "I do not remember much, only that I was the last one standing at the feast. After that...there is nothing."

"Bloodroot then. A Xamidian weed. How it traveled this far from those tepid coasts is a wonder. It constricts the mind and wreaks havoc on the physical body. Is there no honor left in Oitilla?"

Brena's eyes widened in shock. "The duels!" She groaned as she tried to sit up, but was unable. *My body is so heavy.*

"Ho, girl, you will not be fighting in your current state. Your mate or your daughter can take your place in the honor contest."

"Baal has enough on his platter with the chieftain, and Hata is not trained. She did not take a liking to battle."

"*Äiti?*" Hata's head poked in through the hide leather entrance.

"Ho, girl, we were just speaking of you."

"Mother." Hata rushed to Brena's side.

"My daughter," Brena whispered with a weak smile.

"How are you feeling?"

"Exhausted." Brena breathed. "As if a herd of steers has trampled me."

"But that is good, right?" Hata turned to Niemela. "Right?"

"It is good," Niemela answered. "I need to make her another batch of the brew to stave off the poison further." With that, the old healer hobbled away into the other chamber.

"What of your father?" Brena said, straining to get the words out. *I am a sad excuse of a Vouri.*

"Last I saw him, he had gathered a mob, and they were going to overthrow Chieftain Vastaan."

"What!?" Brena again tried to sit up. "The duel was not to be until dusk—" A fit of coughing and pain surpassed her. Forcing her to lie still.

"Do not worry, Father will win. You concentrate on getting better, alright?"

"Oh, my daughter, I fear you are correct. I cannot do anything in my condition. I will have to forfeit my own duel with Alv—" *Alvar!* It came to her like a winter's avalanche. *He offered me a drink. He poisoned the ale. I cannot sit here and do nothing.*

With a scream and a burst of wrath, Brena broke through the pain and came to a seated position. Panting heavily from exertion, she called to her daughter, "Hata, help me up."

"*Äiti,* what are you doing?"

"Ho, girls! What is the meaning of this?" Healer Niemela questioned as she hobbled hurriedly back into the room.

"I know who poisoned me." Brena strained. "Hata, give me your arm."

Reluctantly, Hata did so.

"I do not advise—" Niemela started.

Brena's vision exploded in white...and then darkness.

The war hammer caught Baal's pickaxe with a thundering *clang*. The blow vibrated through his arm. Numbing his hand.

Ota's two-handed parry turned into a full-on downward sweep at Baal's head with the massive hammer.

Baal sidestepped nearly too late, the attack glancing off his shield and cracking into the stone at their feet. The vibrations numbed his entire left arm this time. But he was in close now. *Too close for weapons.* He snarled and smashed his forehead into Ota's face.

Ota reeled back, blood spewing out his broken nose and staining his blonde beard. Blinking with shock, he brought up the shaft of the war hammer just in time to halt Baal's pickaxe from sinking into his chest. The mining tool's sharp end pricked just below Ota's shoulder. Ota bellowed in fury and pushed Baal back.

Baal tried to hold his ground but couldn't find the purchase and was thrown into the crowd of onlookers who caught him as he tumbled into them. They jeered and hollered, pushing him back into the circle of people before the longhouse doors.

Both combatants halted momentarily, panting heavily.

"You are so eager to die, Baal Vasara?!" Ota challenged.

"You poisoned my Brena," Baal hissed in return.

Ota's head tilted questionably. "What are you—"

"You deny it?" Baal thundered, blood pumping in his veins. He surged forward and leaped with two great strides, pulling his arm back to bring the pickaxe down on Ota's skull.

Ota countered with a burst of speed and jabbed the end of the war hammer forward in a two-handed thrust. His reach was longer.

The blue-tinged steel caught Baal mid-air in the center of his gut. Baal gasped for breath as pain shot through him, and the air was pressured out of his lungs.

Ota continued his momentum as Baal grasped at the haft of the long hammer. Ota carried him up and over his head effortlessly. Slamming him into the ground.

Baal's vision blurred and spotted as agony tore at his body. In a daze, he lay still.

"Forfeit, Baal Vasara," Ota said, sucking in extended breaths. "Forfeit and leave Oitilla. Take your family and never return."

Baal groaned and rolled over, spitting blood onto the hard stone ground. Pushing himself to his knees. "I will not submit to such scum as you, Ota Vastaan."

"Then you will die."

He found his feet and wiped the blood from his mouth with a sleeve. Then hefted his pickaxe and shield once more.

CHAPTER SIX

BROKEN

Hata hurried through the streets. The old healer woman had sent her off to find her father. *I feel like an errand boy running back and forth like this. Everyone still treats me like a child. Why did they even get into this stupid argument, anyways? Over some colorful rocks in the ground?*

Some sense itched in her mind. *Almost like footsteps?* She turned just as Dominque crept up behind her.

His bloodshot eyes widened in surprise as she turned, but he continued forward, and too late, she realized as he wrapped his fingers around her neck. She tried with all her might to scream, but nothing came out. She clawed at Dominque's arms, but the stout young man overpowered her. Pulling her off her feet and dragging her toward an alley.

He leaned close to her, his voice spitting venom. "If I cannot have you, nobody will." He began to tear at her garments while atop her now with one hand still gripping her throat.

No, no, no. Not like this. Everything was becoming dark as no air came into her lungs. Then she heard a sickening *thud,* and cool sweet air rushed into her. As her vision cleared, the silhouette of a person stood over Dominque's limp form.

Silja Vastaan stared in shock, tears streaming down her face. "I killed him. I didn't mean to kill him."

A large stone rested in the blood pooling beneath Dominique's body. It had caved in his skull.

"Sil—Silja!" Hata reached out for her. Silja came down to the ground with her, embracing her. They held each other, sobbing in fear, relief, and astonishment.

After some time, they ran. Nobody was about. They ran away from the cooling corpse of Dominique through silent streets. All the way to Hata's home, they ran.

"I cannot believe he would do that to you." Silja panted as they found themselves seated on Hata's bed. "I thought he *loved* you."

"He obsessed over me," Hata said, shaking her head in disbelief. "I thought he was just another typical fool boy. But trying to rape—" the word caught in her throat. She touched the sore parts of her neck where he had strangled her.

"Oh, Hata, I'm so sorry." Silja cupped her face in her hands, staring into her eyes. "Thank Teras I had been looking for you."

Hata looked back into those beautiful eyes. "Thank you, Sil, for saving me."

Silja blushed under Hata's steady gaze. "Of course I saved you. You are the only person in the entire Lân that matters to me."

Hata watched Silja's lips move but did not comprehend the words. Instead, she kissed those moving lips. It was the first time Hata had felt such pleasure and joy. They tenderly undressed one another. The sensation was new and exciting. Silja's soft skin pressed to hers. Finger through her hair. Lips caressing every inch of each other's bodies. *I cannot imagine doing this with anyone else.*

"I love you," Silja whispered.

I've heard those words before. Or that I have known all along. Hata could not contain her smile.

"I love you too."

As Silja lay cradled on Hata's shoulder, relaxing in the bliss of one another's company. Silja suddenly bolted upright. "Your father!"

"What of him?"

"He is fighting my husband as we speak!"

Hata slowly sat up. "I am sure my father stands over the corpse of that old man by now. You are free, Silja. *We are free.*"

"I pray to Teras that you are correct, Hata."

"Then let us go find out."

Blow after blow rained back and forth between the two immense Vouri men. Baal's entire body screamed in agony, yet he did not stop. He did not stop assaulting Ota Vastaan. His arms were deadened and heavy. His legs struggled to take one more step. His lungs burned with exertion. But he strove on. *I will not stop!*

A sweeping arch of the massive hammer came whooshing in. Using the pickaxe and shield as one, Baal batted the blow away. Pain glanced up his arm as his shield began to crack from the countless attacks. But using his momentum, he shoulder rushed into Ota.

Ota grunted in pain as he landed on his back. A breath later, he barely managed to roll out of the way of the sharpened pickaxe raining down on him. The pickaxe sunk deep into the gravel, and Baal struggled to extricate it momentarily. Giving Ota time to recover.

Both men gasped for breath as they faced one another again.

Hata and Silja pushed through the back of the mob. Finally, they came to the open circle. Blood stained the gravel stone beneath both warriors' feet. The silent mob watched in awe as the two men continued an onslaught against one another. Their clothes were tattered and covered in dust, blood dripping from numerous wounds to both men.

Hata whispered to no one in particular, "How long have they been at it?"

"Nearly two bells now," a man said sullenly. "Neither refuse to give."

"By the mountain, we need to stop this." Hata pleaded.

"It is not the way of the Vouri. It will be done when it is done," the man answered.

"Then let me boost my father's confidence." Hata took in a deep breath. With a stomp of her foot, she shouted at the top of her lungs. "Finish him, Isä!" A slight ripple expanded from her feet into the crowd, and the two men locked in battle.

People looked around oddly at the disturbance.

Her father disengaged and followed her voice. When he found her in the mob, he smiled genuinely, blood staining his teeth.

"Finish him, Baal!" the mob echoed her cry.

"Finish him, Baal!"

"Baal! Baal! Baal!"

Silja took up the cry beside Hata.

Baal nodded and turned back to his foe.

Ota Vastaan was not looking at Baal. He glared directly at Silja, who continued to cheer for his adversary.

Hata quickly grasped her arm, pulling it down. "Ota sees you!"

Silja's eyes widened in fear.

Ota raised the war hammer high up above his head and began chanting. "By Teras's might. By Teras's strength. By Teras's stone." His word became louder and louder, drowning out even the cheering of the mob. "By Teras's honor. By Teras's fortitude. By Teras's courage." The runes upon the mighty weapon began to glow with blue light. "By Teras's stability. By Teras's justice."

Her father let out a challenging roar and drove toward Ota.

Ota Vastaan's eye flared with the same blue light as he brought the hammer down. "By Teras's mountain!"

Her father lifted his shield to deflect the attack.

The force of the blow thundered through the cavern, shattering the shield and arm as one.

Baal collapsed to the ground, eyes rolling up in his head. Unconscious.

Hata ran to him. "We give, we surrender," she pleaded to Ota, who towered over them.

"Hata Vasara," Ota breathed, blue vapor swirled out between his teeth. "Gather your pathetic family, leave Oitilla, and never return."

She could not keep her tears back. "Yes, Chieftain, we will go. Let me take him to the healer first."

"I give you only this night. If you all are still within Oitilla come morning"—he grinned a bloody wicked smile—"You will all hang from my rafters." Ota's eyes strayed to Silja. "All of you."

Hata bowed her head. "Very well, Cheiftain."

The mob began to disperse. Murmuring quietly, the people's zeal was thwarted at the fall of Baal.

"Wait!" Alvar Kovaa called out as he came to the circle's center. "Is my challenger ready to contest her claims?!"

The crowd halted and turned back to look.

"She is poisoned and weak. She cannot fight," Hata whispered.

"What's that girl? Speak up." Cheiftain Ota ordered.

"She cannot fight."

"Very well, then both duels are forfeit." Ota waved the crowd away. "Begone!"

Hata watched Ota follow Silja into the longhouse, one massive hand grasped tightly on her slender shoulder. *Will I ever see her again? Can I not even say goodbye? First, I need to get my father to the healer woman.* She gazed about. Her old cart had been pushed aside, but it was still near where she had left it the night before. She fetched it, bringing it to where Baal lay. Try and try as she might, she could not move him. "Can anybody help me?" she called out desperately. "Anybody!?"

The mob was gone.

"I can help you get him loaded," a voice wheezed behind her.

Hata found Alvar Kovaa smiling back at her. His teeth were yellowing and black. *Disgusting. But I have no other choice. "Please,* if you will," she bowed, still gasping from the exertion of trying to move her father's bulk.

"Get his legs then so they don't drag," the soiled miner said as he hoisted Baal from under his arms.

Hata did so, and with Alvar's help, they managed to heave her father into the cart.

"Lead the cart. I'll push from behind," Alvar said.

She couldn't bear his sudden kindness. "Why are you aiding us now? Why did you start this strife to begin with?"

"Why does any sane man do anything? For wealth and power. I have no hard feelings for your family, and Qav's luck to you all."

"My mother and father are both near to death. All for your own greed?"

"Your father started this with his senseless *ill omen*. Blame your father for your family's downfall. Had we simply explored the cavern and found anything untoward, we could have sealed it up and been on our merry ways. But alas, now I am foreman of the mines and will revel in its riches."

"You broke your word."

He merely grinned. "Ah, here we are. We will need to haul Baal up the steps. The cart cannot traverse those."

"Once we get him into the healer's homestead, I never want to see you again."

"And you will not, lass. You will not."

Straining and groaning, they slowly pulled Baal's limp body up the stone steps and into the old crone's hut to lay him next to his mate. Hata's mother was sleeping deeply and did not see Alvar Kovaa standing over her, a smug look of satisfaction on his face.

"Go," Hata hissed.

He did so, and Hata never saw the man again.

CHAPTER SEVEN

VASARA

Brena dreamed of her pursuit of the young man, Baal Vasara. The chase was in full vigor. *I will walk the mountain with that fool of a man! He is not working the mine today. I'll stop by his home.* Baal's father was elderly and sat outside the L-shape homestead, rocking in a chair and smoking on a pipe. His once carroty red beard had gone white, but he had the same shaven head that his son bore.

"Brena Laakso." Niklas Vasara grinned a wide, gap-toothed smile. "Has the fool boy come to understand your courting yet?"

Like many other days, Niklas and she had had this same exchange. "Today is that day. By Teras will, it is," she answered with a chuckle.

"It might do you better to simply beat him over the head with a log."

"Truly I may."

"Well, the big lug is still asleep. Care for a cup of ale?"

"My thanks, that would be wonderful."

"Ah, can you fetch it? It is in the top left cupboard, two cups, if you will."

"Of course." Brena entered the simple home. Baal's name was carved near the end of a long list of words onto the wooden threshold. She spied through a curtain to see Baal snoring like a bear. Then she fetched the cups and ale and pulled one of the wooden kitchen chairs out beside Niklas.

"They say he will make foreman in the next few years at this rate," Niklas said as she seated herself.

Brena poured the dark ale into a cup and handed it to him. "It does not surprise me. He does put his all into the work."

Niklas took a long draught and sighed. "A steady income to raise a family,"

"My thoughts exactly." She drained her cup in one go and poured another.

"We are lucky the Vouri is at peace with Aurulan. There is no need for the warrior caste in Oitilla."

"You are right, but it never hurts to be wary." She bit back some other words. *Niklas is not your typical Vouri. The man is anti-war. He rejects the very teachings of Teras that to die in battle was to honor our people.* She did not want to dispute him, as they were getting along well. Should she blunder with Baal's father, she may lose her chance at Baal himself.

Baal slammed the door open and bellowed, "Drinking without me?!"

"By Teras's stones, the day is half gone, oh son of mine," Niklas answered.

Baal grunted and grinned at her. "Brena. Let us head to the alehouse. Care to join us, *Isä*?"

"You pebbles get a move on then. Let a tired old man rest now."

They did so. Hurriedly, they came to the large square building hiding near the base of Ice Pillar Falls. They took a bench and watched a young lad playing at fisticuffs against a middle-aged, stern-looking man with a salt and pepper beard and long braided hair in the center of the alehouse.

"Ha." Baal snorted, slamming his empty mug to the bench, as the young man took a fist to the face and suddenly went limp. "Witness me, Brena." He stood and sauntered into the ring, towering over the opponent as the young man was dragged away. "My turn."

By Teras, this man.

The grizzled veteran contemplated Baal for a moment and nodded. He took a long draught from a mug someone handed him, then threw it to the ground, raising his fists at the ready.

Baal swung a massive right hook.

The man bobbed beneath it deftly, and like lightning, two jabs struck Baal's stomach and then danced away.

Baal stood unphased; a toothy grin pasted on his face. He roared and, with both hands, tried to slam the man's head between them.

Again, the man ducked and sidestepped away.

"Are you going to fight or are you going to dance like a Xamaidan belly dancer?!" Baal taunted.

Has he ever seen a Xamaidan belly dancer? Brena pondered.

The crowd took up Baal's cry, egging the man to land a blow.

He growled and rushed into Baal's guard. His blows were quick and seemed powerful, yet Baal stood. It was like running face-first into the mountainside.

Baal began to laugh. It was cut short as an uppercut thwacked into his jaw. Suddenly, Baal grasped the man by the wrist he had just connected the blow with. Baal lifted the man from the floor and hissed, "Like I say, now it is my turn." The sound of Baal's upward blow colliding with the man's chin concussed through the chamber.

The veteran went another foot off the ground as his feet went over his head, and he slammed to the wood-planked floor.

"*Viotoon!* Who will be next?" Baal cheered, opening his arms triumphantly.

"I."

Baal turned, and his eyes widened.

Brena let her fur cloak fall to the floor as she entered the arena.

"You jest, Brena? Surely."

"I do not."

He shrugged nonchalantly, then rolled his shoulders menacingly. "Do not say I did not warn you, silly woman."

Brena stretched her arms, then touched her toes. Cracking her knuckles, she fell into her stance.

He came at her with his same wide hook.

Slower than usual. Baal is not taking this seriously. Standing at the same height, she raised her arm and blocked it.

He grinned and continued with a second hook from the other side.

She stood and blocked it.

He blew air from his nostrils and stepped into a powerful cross blow.

Both arms in front of her face, she halted the blow. She smiled back at the fuming man. "Baal Vasara? Is that all you got?"

His face was bright pink as he swung in a rage once more.

Brena inched her head back and let loose a strike on his exposed elbow before her. It caused his forearm to slap in an unnatural direction, and he sucked in a painful breath as that arm fell to his side. She dashed in with a barrage of attacks on his ribcage and abdomen.

He flinched and spasmed at the onslaught. Then he bellowed in anger, his arm seemingly recovered as he grabbed at Brena.

"That's not part of the rules," she whispered as she planted her feet and stepped into a full-on blow to his nose.

His head slammed into the floorboards, and the alehouse erupted in cheers.

Full tankards and a fat purse of coins from those silently betting on her were brought to her. Giving her a cut of the winnings.

Suddenly Baal's laugh rang out in the stuffy chamber.

Brena strode over, looking down at him where he still lay.

His blood-covered face was smiling in delight back at her. "Brena." He offered a hand for her to help him to his feet.

"Baal?" she questioned, pulling him up.

To her surprise, as she lugged him up, he wrapped his arms around her and kissed her.

The cheer erupted once more.

"Brena!" he yelled over the chaos. "Would you walk the mountain with me?!"

Her cheeks ached from smiling. *Well, it's about damned time.*

Brena awoke to the sounds of her husband's muttering.

"I am weak. I am hopeless. I am no Vouri."

"Ho boy, enough sobbing like a child," old Niemela scolded as she wrapped Baal's arm in a tight bandage.

Hata sat at one side of the chamber, head hiding behind her knees and hands. Quiet sobs trickled through.

Brena sat up. More quickly this time. The pain was a faint tension. She queried the room. "What happened?"

"Ho, Hata girl, get your mother a cup from the pot there. Before you depart tonight, I need you to be as fit as possible."

Hata dejectedly did so, filling the cup and bringing it to Brena.

Brena took the cup and finished it with no aid. *I am feeling far better.* "Nobody answered my question." Brena's eyes caught and held her daughter's look.

"Isä lost. He was defeated by Ota," Hata whispered.

There was a moment of stunned silence as Brena comprehended the words. Finally, she laughed. "Ha! Is that all? Your father is not new to losing. For one cannot win every war."

Baal looked up from his muttering.

"Everyone loses at some point. All we must do is learn from it," Brena reassured.

"But we are banished from Oitilla." Hata cried.

"And we are together." Brena reached out and grasped her daughter. "This will be difficult, but we will struggle together. We will meet new people and make new friendships. House Vasara will live on."

Baal stood and stalked over to them. He knelt and embraced them with one good arm. "Your mother is right, my daughter. We will always be together."

They sat in that long embrace until Niemela finally interrupted them. "Ho younglings, the hours are late. Go home, gather what you can and be off. Time is fleeing."

"Our house thanks you, Niemela, for all you have done for us," Baal said. He then helped Brena to her feet and motioned to Hata to lead the way.

Niemela thrust a bundle into Hata's arms. "Take this. Try to make a brew at least twice a day and have your mother drink it. The poison will take a few more days to completely flush from her system."

Hata smiled and nodded and exited the tent.

"There is something special about that one," Niemela said as Brena and Baal followed Hata.

Baal chuckled heartily. "Ha. For she is Vasara. We are all special."

"Yes, yes, boy, now get gone!" Niemela shooed them out the doorway.

Brena sighed contently. *Our spirits are raised, and we will get through this.* Hata placed the bundle in their cart and pulled it home. *She will have a lot of work on the journey down the mountain. I do not think Baal and I can help her pull the cart.* She pondered where they would go as they found themselves at their simple homestead. Slowly, they gathered and packed supplies. Food and water. Extra clothes. Cloaks and blankets. Ale. They decided to trade their goats for a mule at the stables. *We need to hurry. It is well past midnight.*

Baal and Brena lit torches as Hata began to pull the loaded cart back toward the longhouse.

Baal stopped and ran his hand over the carved names on the threshold of their home. "I will carve our name elsewhere, by Teras's mountain, I swear."

"We will carve out a new home, my Baal." Brena reassured him with a hand on his broad back.

He nodded and gave her a toothy smile. "*Joo*, we will, my Brena."

They turned and followed Hata down the road.

Hata let out a blood-curdling shriek as they reached the chieftain's longhouse.

Light from the torches on the front of the building lit up the body of Silja Vastaan. Hung by the neck from the rafters of the longhouse directly over the front entrance. The massive wooden statues stared at her body contemptuously, swaying on the rope.

"Silja! No! No! Sil!" Hata continued screaming and wailing and pounding the ground with her fists.

Brena went to her and tried to calm her, but she could not find the words, and Hata pushed her away.

Finally, Baal picked up his daughter with his good arm, carried her back to the cart, and gently placed her in the back.

They did not notice the sizeable indents in the earth where Hata had slammed her fists.

Then, with that same good arm, Baal pulled the cart. Silently they took their goats and exchanged them in the stable for a mule which they strapped to the cart. All the while, Hata lay amongst their belongings, crying. Slowly, sorrowfully, they crept through the dark, silent streets of their hometown, the village of the Vouri people. The mountain cave town of Oitilla. They weaved down the mountain in the dead of night and headed southeast to follow the edge of the North Iron Belt toward Aurulan and yet further to the Burning Sea.

PART TWO

CHAPTER EIGHT

TOBAK

Baal could not understand the words the people spoke in this little town surrounded by looming, dark pine trees and sparse farming fields. The mountains towering over the little village to the north.

"*Pouvez-vous travailler pour moi*?" The short, fat man with thinning, oily brown hair while holding a sizeable wood-cutting axe grumbled.

"I think he wants you to work for him," Brena suggested.

"Even I could understand that," Baal muttered. "I cannot do it with my arm like this." He winced as he moved his broken left arm slightly.

"Worry not. I will do it." Brena went to grab the axe.

The man pulled it away. "*Pas un travail pour les femmes.*" He turned to leave.

"*Laisse ma mère te montrer sa force,*" Hata called after him.

He came back, shaking his head. Muttering under his breath. But relented and handed the axe over to Brena. He pointed to a pile of thick logs that had been sawed into short pieces. The wood grain was such a dark brown it was nearly black.

It had been nearly two weeks since leaving Oitilla. Brena had recovered completely. She quickly hoisted a heavy log onto a chopping block. She let out a quick 'Rah!' and the axe split through the stump, sending two pieces of timber flying. Nearly striking the fat Auru man.

Baal grinned proudly at his mate. *By Teras's thunder, I am a blessed man.*

"We need...uh," *What are the Auru words again?* Hata pondered. "Shelter? Food?"

"As long as she keeps chopping wood," the rotund man answered, "you all may sleep in the tool shed." He pointed at a small shack at the back of the lumberyard. "Food, you must figure for yourselves."

Hata had to internally repeat the words to fully understand. Dominque had been teaching her the language, but she had not taken it seriously. *I did not think I would ever need it.*

The image of Dominque's blood-thirsty eyes as he wrapped his hands around her throat, forced its way into the mind. Suddenly waves of nausea swept over her, and she hurriedly mumbled, "My family thanks you..." She trailed off as she began to walk toward the little shack.

"Welcome to Tobak," he called after her.

It was a simple building. Tools hung or leaned against the walls. Saws, axes, hammers. Buckets of nails. The floor had a thin layer of hay, but they could lay their fur blankets to rest. *This will do.* Hata stared at the straw, remembering when Silja had first kissed her in the loft of the stables. The flash of Silja's lifeless corpse swinging. The resentment overwhelmed her. *Why did this happen? Why didn't Father win? If he had killed Ota, Silja would still be alive.*

Her father stepped into the shack at that moment. He grunted as he moved about, examining the tools.

Hata could not stand it. "Why didn't you win!?" she screamed at him. Slamming her fists against his chest harmlessly.

His face contorted in shock, then he bowed his head shamefully and whispered, "I am ashamed, my daughter. I failed you. I failed Brena. All the Vouri. I should have died in place of your friend."

"Why did he kill her?" she cried, again slamming her fist against him.

"I am sorry, *tyttäreni.* I do not know." He lifted his one good arm to comfort her but hesitated as she pushed at him.

"I know why." Hata wailed through her tears. Her hands began to ache from the impacts against his solid form. *Why can't you feel my pain!?* "Silja cheered for you in the duel, and *he* noticed. Something as simple as that set him off."

"Is this true?" Baal asked gently.

She nodded her reply, finally resting her head against him.

His hand came up, gently cradling her head. He held her against him, and tears trickled down his face into his beard. "My daughter—" his voice broken. "I love you with all my heart. Unconditionally and forever."

She kept nodding her head into him.

"I will do anything to make this right. If I ever meet Ota Vastaan again, I will kill him."

A few weeks went by in the village of Tobak. The surrounding area, Tobak Forest, was famous for its blackwood pine trees which were premium wood for construction. Brena had been promoted from the woodcutter and now aided in milling the long trunks into beams or planks. *At least the cheap bastard is paying me now.* She hewed into the massive log a team of horses had just pulled in. After marking the tree at a desired depth with a bit of charcoal, she would begin chopping notches across it as roughly as she could to that depth. Then she would knock the chunks between the notches out with a hammer. After which, she would smooth the surface of the beam or plank with a broad axe. Then flip it over and begin the entire process again.

When the lumber was finished, it would be hauled to a metalworker who reinforced the board with iron strips.

Brena wiped the sweat from her brow with a rag. She had torn the sleeves off one of Baal's oversized linen shirts, which hung loosely about her, but let air refresh her body as she strained with the lumber. The perspiration caused her thunderbolt tattoos to glisten in the sun, which in turn was causing passers-by to eye her wearily. *These Auru have never seen a real woman.*

As the thought came to her, a posse of women strolled by with baskets full of clothing and linens. They giggled at the sight of her. All were dressed in heavy-looking dresses of dull colors that hung about their feet.

"She looks like a man." One woman giggled.

"Aye, I fancy a surprise down in her trousers, I do."

The group's snickers died away as they continued toward a stream that edged the village.

Brena sighed as she ladled a drink of water from a bucket. She looked back at the half-hewn log before her. *This is solid, honest work. It keeps me hearty, but by Teras, the day drags on. I do not think this is my calling. I wonder what those two are up to?*

Baal instructed his daughter how to twist the gut tightly. The supplies for simple traps were all they could afford on the small wage Brena was getting from working the logging camp. They had contemplated purchasing a long bow for hunting, but with his arm, it was futile. *I am worthless. Brena is busy working to keep food in our bellies. I cannot expect her to hunt as well. And Hata...*

He studied his daughter. She looked far older since leaving Oitilla. Her face was always sullen. She was not the same smiling girl he remembered from those better days.

"Like this?" Hata asked.

"*Joo*, very good." He nodded. *I do not think she could pull a long bow or score a hit on a wild game. Yet she is good with little things like this, good with her hands.* He watched as she deftly tied three more gut snare traps. "Now let us go set them."

Hata smiled slightly and stood.

Baal groaned as he pushed himself to his feet, his blasted arm still paining him greatly.

"Show me the best spot for them, *Isä*."

They wandered further into the woods. He pointed out some worn grass where small woodland creatures frequented and instructed Hata to nail the gut to a stump or piece of fallen timber they could place near the trails. When the animal ran through, it would be caught and unable to move.

Once they had placed all the traps, they made a wide loop back toward the village. They came to the stream that flowed down toward Tobak. They stopped and ate hard loaves of bread, again all they could afford, and drank deeply from the creek.

As Baal lifted his head from the cool water, there was a rustling in the bushes behind him. He turned slowly. Two large feline eyes watched him.

"Hata," he hissed through his teeth.

She stared at the black-footed lynx as its face emerged from the bushes.

He motioned for her to get behind him. Black-footed lynxes were as big as some enormous dogs, but usually avoided humans. *It must be starved.*

It hissed and lunged toward him, swiping with both clawed forepaws.

Baal let loose a mighty kick as the sharp hooks raked his leg, but the blow collided with the cat's chest and toppled it backward. It screeched and paced back and forth, gauging him

"*Isä!*" Hata yelped from behind him. "Her litter is her in a dead stump."

"By Teras's stone, my girl," Baal exhaled. "Let us move downstream and let the she-cat be."

He crept back, never breaking eye contact with the hissing, spitting mother lynx. Hata placed a hand gently on his back, trying to aid his footing. When they were a reasonable distance out of the way, the lynx sprinted across the creek and into the log.

"Quickly, let us go." He turned and urged Hata on. "We must live on old bread tonight and check on the snares in the morning."

Hata groaned hungrily. "Could we spend mother's wage for a decent meal at the inn tonight?"

Baal's stomach gave a rumbling roar in response to that idea. "Perhaps. We will speak with *Äiti*."

ABIDE

The roasted vegetables melted in Hata's mouth. The mixture of carrots, beans, and potatoes was flavored with a spice she'd never had before. *It is delicious!* The smells made her mouth water even as she spooned another mouthful of the vegetables into it.

Her father rumbled in agreement, as if reading her thoughts as he swallowed the aromatic vegetables.

"That is two days' wages gone." Brena exhaled. "We cannot keep going like this."

"When my arm is healed, I will also work." Baal reassured her.

"How do the rest of the men working the logging camp dine here every night?" Hata pondered aloud, eyeing a group she recognized. The fat, greasy-haired man in their midst.

Her mother followed her gaze. "He pays us and gives us shelter in our need. Let us thank Teras for that."

"We do not need to sleep in the shed," Hata suggested. "If it will pay a higher wage."

"*Joo*, we could camp in the woods," Baal mumbled through a mouthful.

"That is true," Brena answered with a nod. "I will speak with him in the morning. They are well into their cups now."

Still, I do not think he is paying a fair wage. Hata stood. "I will fetch another round of this weedy ale."

"Last one, my daughter," Brena said. "We must save what coin we have left to us."

Hata strode to the barman, tilting an ear to listen to the table full of mill workers. They were speaking fast and drunkenly in Auru, and it was difficult to follow.

"Skrull's balls. The Vouri lass is tall and slender, like a tree," one of the men observed as she walked by.

"Ain't right. Having a lady be taller than yourself just ain't right," another agreed.

"The trio are Skrull damned giants. The man is a monster, and his wife…Have you seen her at the axe? She's on to her third log of the day while I'm finally flipping one over."

"By Qav's coins, and the whore is cheaper than you lot by leagues!" The fat man chortled.

Ah ha. So it is true. Hata gathered her mugs and returned to her parents and sat down. Their platters were licked clean, and they anxiously eyed the new ale at their disposal. She whispered across to them. "He is underpaying you. I just heard him boasting about it."

Both their jaws clenched simultaneously, and their faces reddened.

Oh, by Teras's stones, perhaps I should not have told them yet.

They both stood abruptly. It was like watching a pair of hungry wolves stalking their prey.

"Wait," Hata grabbed at her mother.

Brena pulled free. "At times, my daughter, you cannot let people oppress you. We were raised in the shadow of Teras, and we will stay faithful to His wisdom."

Her father stomped over to the group, and with a guttural bellow, he flipped their table one-handed.

Food and drink splashed about. The group of mill workers yelled in irritation and disgust. Throwing their arms in the air as their clothes were soaked with spilling drinks.

"By all the fucks," one man, the largest of the bunch, pointed a finger up into Baal's face. "What in Skrull's hell are you on about?"

Her father sneered down at the thug.

"What the fuck are you smiling about!?" another shouted. The posse had fanned out and was now surrounding Baal.

"Show him his place, boys," the fat man warbled from a safe distance.

That large man before Baal thudded his fist into her father's smiling face.

He did not move. Still, with his toothy, snarling grin, he clutched the attacker by the neck, lifted him off the floor, and hurled him at the fat man. Both men went sprawling to the ground.

The others shouted and rushed in to assault Baal. One shattered a chair across his back.

Now, with a deep rumbling laugh, her father turned and strode toward the new attacker. The man backpedaled in horror, trying to scramble away but tripped on some debris.

Baal picked him up by the ankle.

Just as the two men lifted themselves to their feet where Baal had thrown them, another body crashed into them.

Her mother came in swinging. Three quick strikes to another assailant sent him to the floorboards, groaning in pain. Another thug grabbed her from behind. She thrust her elbow into his gut, wrapped her arm around his neck, and yanked him over her shoulder. He thudded to the ground.

Hata was too busy watching the destruction of the group of thugs to notice another who had come in the door behind her. The man squeezed her arms tight against her, holding a small knife before her chest.

"Leave off, Vouri bastards!" the voice yelled in her ear. "Or the girl gets it!"

Baal and Brena halted and glared furiously at the new enemy. The veins in her father's neck and head bulged as his chest heaved in rage.

Brena put her hands up to indicate her surrender, touching Baal gently on the shoulder, and whispered in Vouri, "Be calm, my husband." Then in Auru, she said, "We are done. Let her go."

"Move to the door." The knife waved them toward the entrance.

The man moved opposite her parents, still holding her painfully tight. They circled one another.

Teras's stones, I am a burden.

When her parents had their back to the door, her mother spoke again. "We were simply defending our honor. Let her go now."

The fat man yowled at them, holding a hand to his bloodied head. "You aren't welcome in Tobak anymore, barbarian bastards. We should slit the girl's throat."

Brena's fiery glare burnt into the man as she said calmly, "If you do so, you will all die this day."

The group murmured anxiously amongst themselves. Finally, the man holding Hata released her and nudged her forward.

She ran to the waiting arms of her mother.

"Get out of Tobak," the fat man wheezed. "Get out of my shed."

Baal grumbled in broken Auru, "C...crush heads?"

The men stirred restlessly.

Brena chuckled, but stopped Baal. "They are not worth it."

With that, the family left the murky tavern.

"I'm sorry," Hata whispered as they loaded their few belongings into their cart.

"Daughter, you discovered their deceitfulness. We thank you," her father said, patting her back.

"I think the Vouri way is not always the wisest in hindsight." Brena sighed. "We could have approached the situation differently, my mountain."

"No," her father grunted in disagreement.

Her mother sighed and stretched. "Well, I was getting tired of chopping wood, anyway. That little bout was refreshing."

"It is time we moved on," her father announced. "Let us move into the woods to camp, as it is already late. I want to gather the traps before we set out in the morning."

Hata followed silently. *I am no help to them. My parents are warriors, and I am weak. I wish I could help somehow.*

Chapter Ten

DEPENDANT

Baal awoke to the sounds of people trudging through the woodlands. He silently peered through the trees. He recognized the man from a few nights ago. The man who had put a knife on his daughter. He had dark chestnut hair tied tight in a ponytail and a stubbly beard broken white by a long scar from his ear to his chin. He strode with a lightness to his step. *This man is no ordinary thug,* Baal thought. Dangling over the man's shoulder were two fat hares, dead, caught in snares. *Our snares.* He was surrounded by a group different from the tavern ordeal. These were dressed in leather armor and carried long hunting bows, daggers, and short swords. *Mercenaries?*

Baal, keeping as low as he could, retrieved one of his pickaxes. He had packed a few in case they came across a mine he could find work in. He then nudged his mate's foot with the end of the pickaxe.

Brena blinked tiredly, but was soon crouched beside him when she saw his sullen expression. "What is it?"

"The man from the tavern," he whispered, pointing through the trees. The group was not moving toward them, but at an angle. They were not silent, and Baal could hear them breaking branches and prattling as they went. "I think they stole the traps I set last night. Two fat hares."

"That would have been our food for a day and a bit." Brena crept to the cart and extracted her longsword and shield. "How many were there?"

"Ten, I counted. But the Auru bastards have weapons."

Brena stopped.

He watched her eyes fall on Hata, still sleeping silently. It dawned on him as well. *Ten men are a lot to handle. I am not worried for my Brena and me. But…*

Hata groaned and rolled restlessly.

"Perhaps, my mountain," Brena suggested gently. "Perhaps this is such a time we must think before we act."

Baal closed his eyes and breathed deeply through his nose. *She speaks true.* He smiled at Brena and then shrugged. "So we go hungry today. I only saw two of the snares. Let me go check the third."

Sometime later, Baal looked down on the scrawny squirrel dead in his snare.

A handful of days crept away as they followed a well-trodden path indented by wagon wheels and riddled with horseshoe prints. They'd not met anyone on the road that skirted the mountain range, and they followed it in a southeastern direction. Water was abundant as streams were plentiful, coming down from the North Iron Belt. Hata had spotted a bush of wild blackberries, and they were overjoyed at the find, along with a pile of acorns, which they boiled to soften them. The slightly sweet, slightly bitter nuts were quite satisfying when combined with the tart berries.

"Will we stop at the next village?" Hata pondered aloud.

"It is the most sensible option," her mother answered as she pulled the cart onward. "We must find work, not only to survive but to start anew."

"*Joo*, perhaps I simply cut this useless arm off?" her father suggested, a heavy note of irritation in his voice.

"It will heal soon," Brena reassured.

"I will find work as well," Hata added eagerly. "Even if it is serving ale at a tavern."

Her mother said nothing as she continued pulling the cart, but her father smiled and nodded at her. "That would be an honor to our house, my daughter."

Brena turned her head. "You must take care of lecherous men."

"I will stay nearby since I cannot do much else," her father reassured his spouse.

"That would be well, I think," Brena said.

"You do not need to watch me like a child," Hata said. "I am a grown woman."

"Hata Vasara. It is a dangerous Lân." Her mother scolded her. "We all must be careful!"

That is the first time she has raised her voice at me since childhood. Hata realized.

Baal was looking at Brena with a dumbfounded look as well.

Her mother breathed deeply. "Home in Oitilla. We were safe. We let you do as you please, learn, and pursue whatever you wish. We did not force you to take up the sword, but now I look back with regret at that decision. Out here, we only have each other. We *must* protect each other."

I know she is right, of course. Still, I am twenty summers old. I can take care of my— Dominque's hands gripped her throat. The man poked his knife toward her heart. *No.* She shook her head in more comprehension. *No, I cannot take care of myself. I cannot protect myself from any man strolling down the road who would have the inkling to use his power to take me.* Hata shuddered at the thought, her gut twisting with fear. After walking in silence for a long time, Hata finally answered her mother. "*Äiti*, I will listen. I will be careful and stay near to *Isä*."

"Worry not, my daughter." Her father chuckled. "If any man so much as brushed a finger against you, he will not be able to use those fingers again in this life."

I would feel secure if he was keeping an eye out.

The sun was near setting when a town peaked into sight in the distance. The dim glow of lanterns and firelight blinked into existence as the dusk grew into the night.

"Perhaps we should make camp outside of town," her mother endorsed. "Trying to find lodging in the darkness of night does not seem logical."

"And we do not want to make another scene at a tavern while the patrons are drunk," Hata added.

"It is for the best," her father agreed.

They turned off the road and found a secluded patch of bushes and trees to find rest.

Chapter Eleven

BOLSTER

Brena breathed in the smell of fresh air. The morning had come, and the trio entered the quaint little town. It was a valley of fertile rolling hills and vast patches of farmland. Vibrant, leafy green crops were grown nearly knee-high as spring was well on its way out. An orchard of apples stretched over the hills to the south. Cattle could be seen grazing to the north. Low picket fences marked off the separated fields.

A low stone wall seemed to border the entire village as they approached. As they advanced, a man popped out from behind a large hedge on one side of the wall. Dressed in a dirty tan shirt and torn brown trousers.

"Halt," he ordered, holding a pitchfork at the ready.

Brena held up her hands reassuringly. "We mean you no harm. We are travelers seeking food and shelter for a night or two." *My Auru has developed well since working at the logging camp.*

"How do I know you ain't working for those brigands? The lot of you look right vicious."

"Brigands?" Brena questioned with a look of disgust. "Ha! By Teras's thunder! We are Vouri. We do not dishonor our names by resorting to thieving and murder out of greed."

"Vouri, you say?" The man studied each of them in turn. "I've heard you mountain people are uncontested in battle. They say a squad of Vouri held a mountain pass against the thousands of the Auru of old."

"Indeed." Brena nodded at her husband. "My mate is a direct descendant of Megin and Kol of House Vasara. The two and a handful of others fought against the forces of Aurulan hundreds of years ago. They held the pass and forced the invaders back. We never retaliated into Aurulan as we long to be in the mountains."

"Skrull's sodden balls, I've never heard it told that way. They always say the winters and ice of the peaks drove back the invasion."

"That had a factor in it. It is true, but it is not the tale as a whole."

Hata leaned close to her father and asked in Vouri, "How have I never heard this story before?"

"What story?" He grunted frustratedly. "I cannot follow the conversation. They speak too quickly. I heard Megin and Kol. The story of my ancestors and holding the gorge?"

"Not much to tell. The Auru hounds ran with tails between their legs at the slaughter of their kin."

Brena cleared her throat. "Perhaps we can aid you in your troubles?"

"Thank the Primus." The man began nodding repeatedly. "We could use the help. Welcome to *La Vierge*."

He escorted them to a sizable town square. A few market booths dotted the courtyard, bare and abandoned. A large temple with doors wide open loomed on one side. The sound of pained agony drifted out of the sanctuary.

"We have been harassed once a week for the last month. The bastards wound and pillage our people. Taking crops and even cattle for themselves. Our priestess of Hettra does what she can to tend to the hurt, but as someone finally gets back on their feet, two more are taken in after another attack."

"My daughter will help with the wounded." Brena waved Hata over. "She has stitched our bodies on many occasions."

"*Joo*, I can help with that," Hata said.

"By all means," the man answered. "Speak with Priestess Amahle. She will tell you what needs to be done."

Hata nodded and hurried into the large building.

"When will the bandits attack next?" Brena queried.

"You just missed them, actually. I would reckon another week before they return."

Brena turned to Baal and spoke in their own language. "Speaking of Megin and Kol, shall we enact the same strategy against these brigands? Bring them to a choke point and drown them in their own blood?"

Her mate smiled eagerly, huffing his chest in anticipation. "Aye, my Brena. That would do well."

She turned to the farmer. "We have a plan, but I did not get your name?"

"Aaron Marion," the man answered. He was young, perhaps in his late third decade.

"Well, Aaron Marion, here is what we must do..."

Hata squinted into the gloom of the temple and covered her nose against the rank air. Oak pews had been pushed against one wall while people lined the floor covered in bloody bandages and smelling of death. A massive stained-glass window had been shattered at the far side, and bits of crimson and violet glass dangled from metal frames still attached to the wall.

Hata peered about the room. "Priestess Amahle?" she called out.

A door squeaked open further back in the room, and a tall woman of Tal'tulu descent rushed into the chamber. Her robes were stained with blood and grime. Her dark face was gaunt with fatigue. Curly black hair with a hint of gray was tied up high on her head.

"What is it, lass? Are there more wounded? Surely they have not attacked again so soon?"

"Oh, no, madam. I, uh, have been sent to help you."

"It be blessings from the Primus Himself. Why didn't you say so?" Priestess Amahle beckoned her to follow. "Come, come."

The woman's slight accent caused Hata to deliberate over the words more than usual as she followed.

They entered a small back room that looked like it used to be a kitchen. Two people lay on a large table. A young boy with a gouge partially stitched on his arm. And a woman with a piece of bone jutting out of her shin.

"Can you stitch?" Amahle asked.

"*Joo*...I mean, yes."

"Finish the lad's arm, then. I'll be tending to this one."

Hata took a deep breath as her fingers took up the hooked needle dangling where the priestess had left it. Blood oozed out of the cut as she squeezed it and punctured the skin. The boy groaned. Hata felt slightly dizzy, but she had seen this before.

I have done this a thousand times for Father and Mother after hunts, tavern brawls, fisticuffs, and mining injuries. It is nothing new.

She clenched her teeth and continued.

There was a resounding *crack,* and the woman on the table next to her screamed in agony. Her eyes rolled back in her head as she fell unconscious.

"Ah ha, now it is set, eh," the priestess said warmly. She then tied two solid straight sticks to either side of the calf and wrapped it tightly. She then came to where Hata worked and leaned over her shoulder.

"Done," Hata said just as the priestess began to inspect.

"Hettra's sagging tits, my lass. You did well. Quick like, too."

"My parents like to fight."

The priestess finally took a moment to look Hata up and down. "You are Vouri, correct? Your kind rarely comes down from the mountains."

Hata's head fell. That flash of Silja hanging. She whispered through clenched teeth, "We do not do so willingly. My family has been *coerced* to leave."

"Ah, leave it at that, lass." The woman patted her on the shoulder. "I ain't been home to Tal'tulu in nearly three decades. Though I miss the white sand in my toes and the warm ocean breeze on my skin sometimes."

"Where are you from?" Hata cleared her throat politely. "I've never met anyone who didn't look like me and my kind before. The Auru people are very similar."

"Ah, lass, you Vouri be quite secluded up in those peaks, eh?" Amahle guided her into yet another room with a small bed and a desk. On the desk was a loaf of bread and a jar of honey. Amahle cut the loaf, spread the creamy honey atop a piece, and handed it to Hata.

"Oh no, you don't have to feed me—"

"Nonsense, girl. Take it and eat. The honey is fresh from our field bees."

Hata took a small bite. *It is so sweet.* She quickly devoured the portion.

"My people come from far to the east," the priestess said. "Far across the Earste Lân. Across the desert of the Burning Sea, past the brilliant coastal cities of Xamid. There is a scattering of islands out in the Sea of Xamid. The Isles of Tal'tulu. This is where my people be calling home. But these days, many of us live in Aurulan and Xamid alike. As a child, my father brought me here to start anew. I found my calling under the guidance of Hettra. The rest is history."

"By the mountain. I feel like I have been living under a stone."

Amahle chuckled. "That is quite an accurate description of your situation, lass."

"I wish to see Tal'tulu one day."

"Well, my young friend, if the Primus One wills it, you may one day find your own toes in those warm white sands."

She scoffed internally. *Like some made up god would have a say in it. Primus One...Teras, cast him down your cliff.*

Chapter Twelve

PASSION

"That temple is the most advantageous position to stage an ambush," Brena said to the gathering of the townsfolk. "I propose we inform the bandits that we have surrendered and tell them we have gathered food and money for them to take within the temple."

Nervous glances and murmurs expressed about the sullen faces of the townsfolk. There were about two dozen or so who were fit enough to stand.

"My mate and I." Brena gestured to her husband, who stood beside her menacingly. "We will attack those brigands who enter the temple. The rest of you will scatter yourselves within the other buildings around the town square. Now, no one needs to fight if they do not wish, but once we have sprung our trap, we will do all we can to route the enemy quickly. That being said, there will still be some enemies out here, and when they discover what is going on, they may attack any of you who would be close by."

"I will speak with the brigands," Aaron said. "I will lead them to the trap. Someone must do it."

Brena saw Baal nod and grin widely at the brave farmer. "*Voitoon*, Aaron!" Baal thumped his one good hand to his chest.

"For this not to raise suspicion, you cannot all be in hiding. Some must be present in the square for the bandits to see. Those can carry small weapons to surprise the bandits if they deem to join the battle. Remember, the element of surprise is on your side. They will not expect you all to suddenly attack. Are there any hunters among you?"

"Old Colin knows how to bend a bow," a man, well into his sixth decade, answered.

"Think you can score a hit once the avalanche begins?" Brena asked.

"Aye, lass, I have been taking buck at a hundred paces since your ma has been wiping your arse."

Chuckles rippled through the onlooking peasants.

"*Joo*, good." Brena nodded. Then she addressed them all, slowly raising her voice as she said, "I beseech all else who take up hiding nearby. Have whatever weapon you can muster at the ready. At the ready to take up the defense of *La Vierge*."

"*Voitoon!*" Baal bellowed.

"To victory!" Brena called out after him.

"To victory!" the group of ragtag men and women answered the call.

A few days had passed since their arrival in *La Vierge*. Her parents were meticulously planning their attack with the villagers. Hata carried the back end of the stretcher as Amahle took the front. *We need to move everyone before the bandits come.* They were now using a few homes on the village's far side from where Aaron had said the brigands usually came from, to care for the wounded. She breathed heavily as they gently lay the woman with the broken leg on the floor. They gently picked her off the stretcher and transferred her to a pile of straw covered with a relatively clean sheet of linen on the floor near the homestead hearth.

"That was the last one." Hata breathed deeply, then took a long swig from her waterskin that hung at her waist. *It is good to finally be helpful since my life became without order.*

Amahle answered with a content sigh, as if reading Hata's thoughts. "Does the heart well to be helping others in need, my dear girl."

Her lips curled into a smile at the woman. "It does." Amahle was near her parents' age, but Hata couldn't help but find the woman beautiful.

Amahle caught her staring. "Something on your mind, girl?"

Hata blushed. "I'm sorry. I just find you to be a lovely human being, is all."

"Hettra's love to us all." The priestess blessed her. "Regrettably, the apostolic of the Primus One looks down on those who express their love to anyone other than the opposite gender. But you know, there are good things and wrong things about any religion. I follow Hettra because She tells us to love everyone, with all their differences."

"What are you saying?"

"I'm telling you to pursue *your* love, no matter what anyone tells you is right or wrong."

Hata nodded and, still blushing, said, "Well, I uh...find you *intriguing*."

"And I thank you for your attention, but..." Amahle paused, watching Hata's expression fall at the word 'but.' She chuckled. "Everyone be experiencing rejection at some point, girl. As a Priestess of Hettra and, furthermore, the Primus One, I must resist such indulgence."

"Resist, you say?" Hata bit her lip.

"Skrull's balls, girl, your charms will not work on me, eh." Amahle snorted as she guided Hata from the small homestead. "Come, those bastard brigands will be here tomorrow. We must make sure everything is set within the temple."

Baal passionately embraced his mate. He sat on the edge of a solid bed as Brena wrapped her legs about him. His hand weaved through her loose blonde hair that curtained about her body as he traced the dark thunderbolt tattoos up her bare back. They pressed into one another tenderly, gradually...but their hunger began to heighten.

With a gasp, her nails raked against his back as stimulation quickened. He growled as she grasped his throat and bit at his lip.

Baal stood with a growl and lifted her one-armed.

She clung to him, taking him.

They walked. They ran. They panted, groaned, and sweat *together* as they reached the mountain's peak.

Chapter Thirteen

OUTLAW

Sébastien Dubois led his band of outlaws into the town of *La Vierge*. His band had scouted out this town for pillaging a few months back. *La Vierge* had no instated town guard, making pickings easy for him and his crew. *The poor fucks, but a man's got to do what a man's got to do. This is safer by far than my days in the army.*

"Time to sit back and enjoy the plundering, boys," he called out as they strolled toward the little stone fence surrounding the town.

His band cheered and laughed.

A man appeared from the entrance to the town, hands up in submission.

Well, this is new...the peasants would at least try to resist our incursions before. Sébastien shrugged. "Looks to be like they're tired of struggling. Shall we see what he has to say?"

His troop snickered and hooted again, drawing weapons as they approached.

"We have had enough," the peasant man called out. "We have gathered our goods as tribute. Just let our people go unscathed."

Well, you cannot blame them. Sébastien strode up to the young peasant man, a friendly smile on his face as he did. *I'll give the fuck credit for his bravery.* The farmer stood firmly, but his eyes darted nervously to each of Seb's men.

"Please, sir—"

Seb thudded his fist into the man's gut. The man gasped and keeled over Seb's arm. He then slammed his elbow into the man's back, sending him to the ground.

The peasant rolled over, groaning in pain. "W...why," he hissed through ragged breaths.

"We accept your tribute, but alas, my boy..." Sébastien Dubois crouched down, drawing a dagger from his belt; he pricked just below the eye of the man and slowly dragged the point downward. The man did not scream, but his face contorted as the blade cut him. Sébastien sighed as he finished his handy work. "We can't be letting you all go *unscathed*. 'Tis bad for our repute, see."

The farmer grasped his face with his hand, trying to stop the blood flow.

"Come now, it won't be as bad as this." Sébastien pointed to the scar curved from his ear to his chin. "Got this serving our high and mighty King, I did. At any rate..." He motioned to two of his men. "Get him on his feet." Clovis and Andre quickly lifted the peasant to his feet. "Now, boy, show us this tribute."

Clovis nudged the man forward. He said nothing as he stumbled along.

Sébastien studied the quiet homesteads. Shutters were closed and barred. A linen sheet moved slightly across a window as they approached the town square. *Good, stay in your homes, cowards. We'll come a knocking after gathering this so-called tribute. I reckon I saw a ripe young lass or two. The boys and I can have some fun with the whores. Even take 'em back to camp, this time as collateral for the following tribute.*

As they strode into the town square, a handful of peasants huddled together near the shabby old tavern.

The old Tulu priestess gasped and hurried to the young farmer, pulling a rag from her waist and holding it to his face. "Why you be doing such a thing?!" she demanded of Sébastien, stepping up to him. "We yield."

"Aye, ya did." He backhanded her across the face.

She twisted and fell to the dirt. The crowd of peasants gasped and muttered, shifting about nervously.

"She is mighty old, but I reckon the old cunt can't still handle a cock." He nodded at his man, Jules, to restrain her.

"Wait!" the young farmer shouted, pointing at the temple. "Your tribute is within. What little food, wine, and coin we have left is stacked there."

This is too easy. Sébastien smirked and nodded to three of his men to go check it out. Forgetting momentarily about the priestess.

"Drinks are on me, lads," Clovis shouted as he hurried into the temple.

Andre leaned close to Sébastien's ear. "That ginger looks like she needs a good fuck, eh boss?"

Ginger? He had not seen a ginger lass on their previous jaunts to *La Vierge.* He scanned the crowd of peasants, and in their center, he saw the girl. *The Vouri bitch from Tobak.* The people of Tobak did not know he was a brigand, and he had regularly visited the small logging town for a taste of beer and honest conversation once in a while. The image of the two Vouri warriors effortlessly wreaking havoc among a large group of solid men returned to him. *Why is she here? Where are her parents?!*

It dawned on him too late. "No! Stop!" he started to call, stepping toward the large temple just as the screams resounded from it.

Skrull's hell broke loose the next few seconds. An arrow thudded into the back of the man standing next to him. One of his men ran out of the church, missing an arm. The blonde Vouri women rushed behind him, skewering him through the gut and kicking him to the dust.

The massive bald man charged past her, blood dripping down his face into a wild, toothy grimace.

Sébastien's nearest man, Jules, stood dumbfounded, standing over the priestess who lay at his feet. He raised a short blade against the massive man.

The pickaxe caused Jules's head to explode.

Sébastien back-stepped. "What are you standing around for, you fucks? Kill him!"

The sound of fighting came from behind him. He turned to see a handful of peasants stabbing and chopping with pitchforks, sickles, and axes. Overwhelming two more of his men immediately. *Moreau and Landry.*

The other group of peasants huddled in the square charged forward in a mob, minor knives, and tools appearing in their hands from their raggedy clothing.

What in Skrull's hell is happening?! Sébastien turned and sprinted away, shouting over his shoulder to his last two men, "Lucien! Antoine! By all the fucks! Run!"

Two peasants stood before Sébastien.

An old man was drawing an arrow back, his arm shaking at the effort.

Sébastien Dubois flicked a dagger out from his belt. It twirled through the air and sunk into the geezer's chest. The old bastard's eyes widened as he loosed the arrow. It whistled past Sébastien's ear.

The other was a middle-aged woman, nervously holding a sickle.

He rushed in, ready to finish her quickly.

Something crashed into him from the side. White exploded behind his eyes as he hit a wall of one of the buildings. Breaking through the flimsy boards and plaster. Pain coursed through Sébastien as he tried to push himself up. A grip tightened on his leg like iron manacles and pulled him from the wreckage. He twisted onto his back, grasping for another dagger. He looked up at the blood-soaked visage of the bear-like man. Dark thunderbolt tattoos cresting his dripping head.

Is his beard red-colored, or is it simply from all the gore?

Sébastien managed to wrap his hand around his short sword and swing it at the man's arm. The man did release him, but with a roar, his other arm broke free from a sling, and both hands were suddenly on Sébastien's head, lifting him from the ground. Fingers dug into his skull like no pain he had ever felt before. White stars began to burst in his vision. He swung his blade at the man weakly. Sébastien scored another handful of cuts, but the man growled and tightened his grip further.

The man let up for a moment, spitting blood into Sébastien's face. In broken Auru, he roared, "No...touch...my...daughter!"

Skrull's fucking hell. I should have stayed in the army...

Chapter Fourteen

ONWARD

Hata watched as the scar-faced man fell at her father's feet, his head crushed like a melon.

The townsfolk erupted in a cheer over the bodies of ten dead bandits.

Later that night, after the bodies had been cleared away, and the dirt smothered over the bloodstains, the village of *La Vierge* built a massive bonfire in the square. They played music, and caskets of wine were tapped and poured out for all. People danced around the fire, celebrating their freedom from the brigands. Food was brought, and everyone filled their bellies. Hata and her family were bombarded with praise, thanks, and an endless drizzle of wine into their tankards.

They drank and ate and enjoyed their period in *La Vierge*. A few weeks stretched by. Hata tended to the wounded until all were healed. Her mother trained the townsfolk in combat. Her father's arm was on the mend, but he needed to let it rest again after using it against the bandit leader. The people fed and housed them but had little else to pay the family for their help. In the end, her parents decided it was best to move on.

"There is a town on the edge of the Burning Sea that is said to be prospering with trade and work for folks such as yourselves," Aaron said as they readied to set out. "Dagad was the name."

"Our thanks to you, Aaron." Brena firmly grasped him on the shoulder. "May Teras grant you and your people his fortitude in what is to come."

They bid farewells and trekked parallel to the mountains in a southeastern course. As the days continued, the range slowly dwindled in foothills. The woods receded, the rolling hills lost their lush sheen, and the vegetation became rigid and sparse. Long patches of yellowing grass scattered the area. The air was dry, and the ground took on a red-brown color.

Many people traveled the road from the large town they glimpsed in the distance. Snaking rows of wagons and carriages full of goods and people trickled by as their mule pulled their cart into the village of Dagad. Across a bridge over a low muddy river. Hundreds of square beige buildings emerged from a colorful market street of canvas-covered shops.

Her parents were hired immediately for numerous jobs around town, such as bodyguards, bouncing at one of many local taverns, or general physical labor. Hata found work doing laundry and other small housekeeping tasks for many of the well-off citizens of Dagad. Eventually, they were afforded a small homestead, and life continued on. Until one day, Hata Vasara met a merchant in the market offering her samples of his smelling salts...

EPILOGUE

Alvar grimaced as Ota Vastaan looked over his shoulder as he worked. Pulling a large chunk of stone away from the rubble-strewn wall, a crimson light washed over them. *You did not need to come and watch me work, chieftain,* Alvar seethed internally. *Now I cannot steal any jewels for myself.* He slammed into the rock again, chipping away, expanding the opening.

"Can you work any faster, little man?" Ota grumbled.

Alvar turned in annoyance. "I'm working as quickly as possible. You could stop standing around and take up a shovel."

Ota smirked wickedly. "This work is far below me. Besides, I cannot even lift so much as a shovel." Ota touched one of the many bandages wrapping his head and body.

"Have it your way. Just be silent and let me work."

The sounds of rubble moving and pebbles rustling on stone echoed behind Alvar. *From the hole.* He turned to see a hideous face staring back at him, glowing yellow eyes, long protruding fangs, and matted black fur. A massive, deformed clawed hand shot out, piercing Alvar through the throat.

Alvar gurgled and wheezed as he was lifted from the ground, his head lulled, and he saw the upside-down silhouette of Ota Vastaan retreating down the tunnel. As the creature tore into his chest with its jaws, Alvar Kovaa had one last thought.

It indeed was an ill omen, Foreman Vasara...

AFTERWORD

This short novella doesn't end here. It picks up again, with Hata and family right at the beginning of the first book in the main series, The Shepherds of the Sunstone. If you want to find out what happens next please pick up a copy!

THE SUNSTONE SAGA

How Reviews Help

As an independent or self-published author, marketing and promoting my business is ultimately out of my pocket. One of the most incredible things a reader can do to help with this is to leave a review. This will help other readers interested in buying my books and give me more visibility in the marketplace to help advertise them for me.

If you liked *Caste of the Mountain,* please consider leaving me a review!

Caste of the Mountain

Thank you for your support!

About the Author

Nicolin lives in the Greater Toronto Area with his wife and two daughters, writing books, drinking beer, gardening, or shoveling snow.

For more information:

www.nicolinodel.com

nicolinodel@nicolinodel.com